SUPERTATO

KU-526-969

For my lovely Dad

Thank you to Wanda Linnet for her robot picture

SIMON AND SCHUSTER
First published in Great Britain in 2014
by Simon and Schuster UK Ltd
1st Floor, 222 Gray's Inn Road, London, WC1X 8HB
A CBS Company

Text and illustrations copyright © 2014 Sue Hendra
By Paul Linnet and Sue Hendra

The right of Sue Hendra to be identified
as the author and illustrator of this work
has been asserted by her in accordance with
the Copyright, Designs and Patents Act, 1988

All rights reserved, including the right of reproduction
in whole or in part in any form

A CIP catalogue record for this book is available
from the British Library upon request

978-1-4711-2265-1 (HB)
978-1-4711-6346-3 (PB)
978-1-4711-2225-5 (eBook)

Printed in China
3 5 7 9 10 8 6 4 2

SUPERTATO

by Sue Hendra

SIMON AND SCHUSTER

London New York Sydney Toronto New Delhi

Some vegetables are frozen for a very good reason. Don't believe me? Then keep reading.

It was night-time in the supermarket and all was quiet. But –

crash, bang – something had escaped from the freezer.
Something small and round and green.

Something looking for trouble.
Big trouble.

"Help! Help!" cried Carrot. "I'm stuck to the conveyor belt!"

"Aargh!" cried Broccoli. "Someone's drawn on my face!"

"Hmmmmpfff!" cried Cucumber.

Who was doing this? And was there anyone who could help these vegetables in distress?

He used his
super speed . . .

He used his
super strength . . .

He used a flannel
and some soapy water.

"I know who's behind this," said Supertato.
"There's a pea on the loose!"
"Oh no – not a pea!" everyone gasped.

"Yes, a pea! But I'm out of the freezer now and I'm never going back! Mwah ha ha ha ha!" And the evil pea ran off to commit more terrible crimes.

"Time for a dip, little veggies!"

"That's enough!"
shouted Supertato.

He leapt towards
the pea, but the pea
popped out of his
hands and vanished
into thin air.

Supertato set out on a super search.
He crept through the cakes . . .

checked the cheese . . .

and snuck up on the beans.
Then something
caught his eye.

"The game's up!" yelled Supertato.

KERPOW!

But the pea bounced out of reach and onto a trolley. Supertato was just about to stop him with his super strength

when the trolley crashed –

and he was thrown down into
the icy depths of the freezer.

Was this the end for Supertato?

GASP!

Not quite.

But the pea was off his trolley
and lying in wait.
"You're finished, Supertato!"
he shrieked.

But Supertato summoned up
all his strength . . .

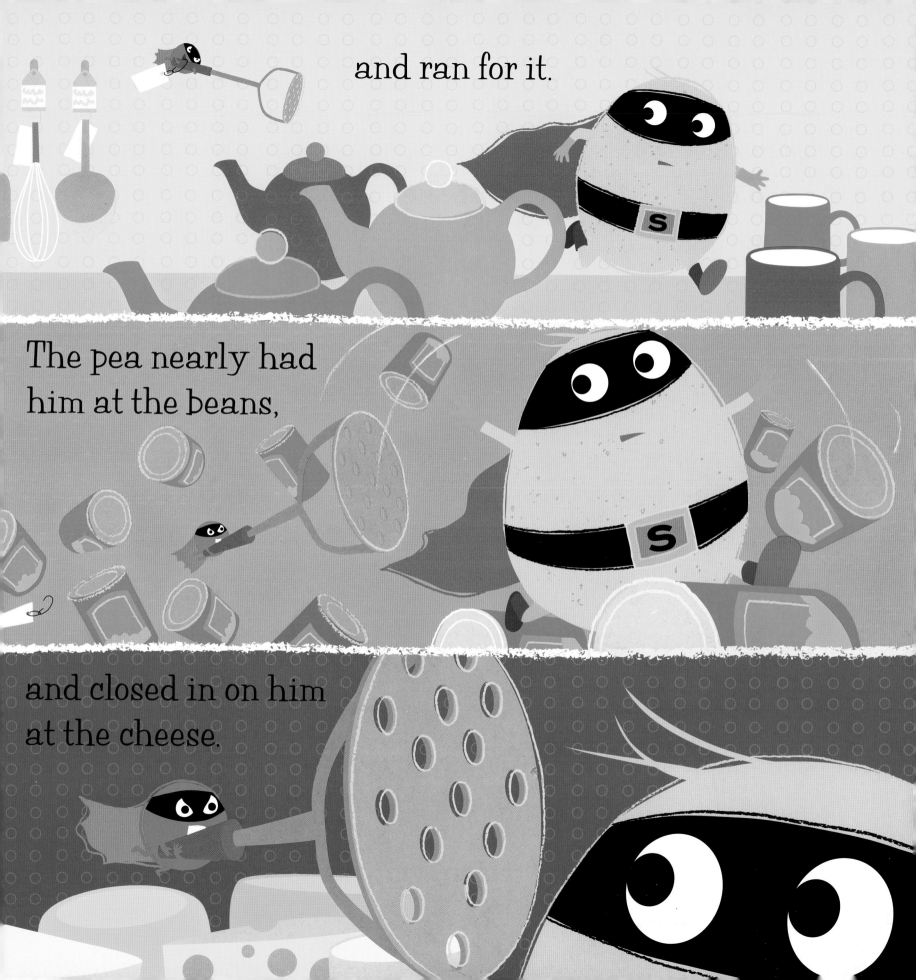

and ran for it.

The pea nearly had
him at the beans,

and closed in on him
at the cheese.

He had him cornered at the cakes.

"So much for Supertato!" screeched the pea. "You're about to be MASHED POTATO!"

Surely THIS was the end for Supertato?

"Not today, my friend," said Supertato.

"Gotcha!"

"Mmmppfff!" said the pea.

SQU

"Oh yes," said Supertato. "I set my trap and you fell for it. Or should that be IN it?!" And he grinned a super grin.

Supertato had saved the day.
"Take him away," he said.
And the pea was marched back
to the freezer where he belonged.

"This jelly tastes of pea!" said Broccoli. And everybody laughed and cheered.

So, remember, folks . . .

Some vegetables are frozen for
a very good reason. Maybe you'd
better go and check your freezer. Just
in case there's an escapee in your house . . .